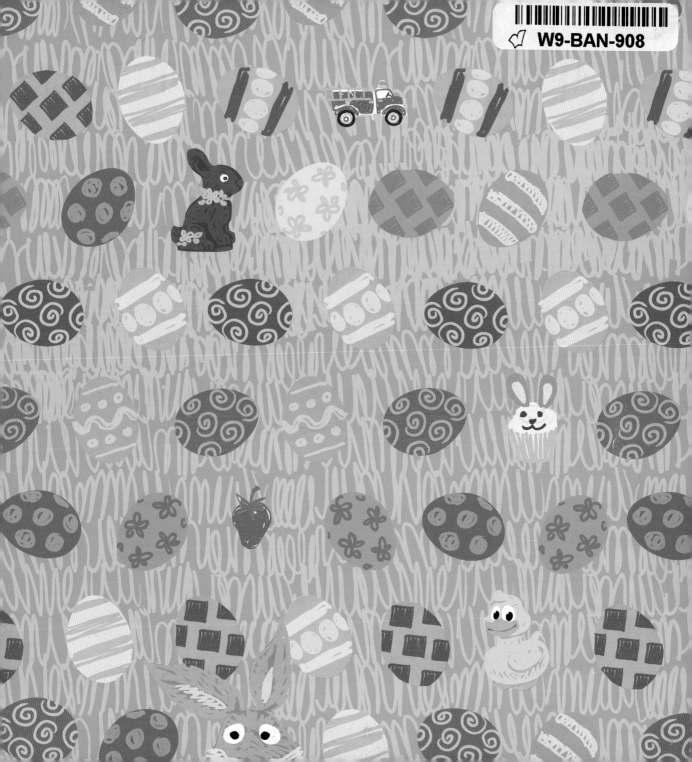

Happy Easter Emmett!

Ashley, Ovi, & Damen

LOVE YOU ♡

The GREAT EASTER RACE!

By Craig Manning   Illustrated by Ernie Kwiat

sourcebooks
jabberwocky

It was a bright Easter morning on Sesame Street,
and out in the park, friends were starting to meet.

There were beautiful colors and flags waving free.
Something special was happening. But what could it be?

"A race!" shouted Big Bird. "Come one and all, the young and the old, the short and the tall."

"Let's stretch out our legs and tie up our shoes. Get ready, get set, there's nothing to lose!"

The park's woodland creatures, they all heard the yell
(and a little green turtle popped out of his shell).

"May *we* join the race?" they asked all together.
"Of course!" Big Bird said. "*More* makes it *better*!"

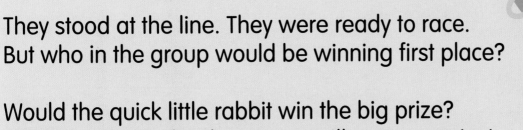

They stood at the line. They were ready to race.
But who in the group would be winning first place?

Would the quick little rabbit win the big prize?
Keep an eye on that bunny—you'll get a surprise!

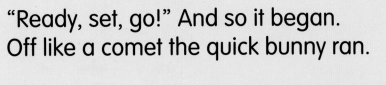

"Ready, set, go!" And so it began.
Off like a comet the quick bunny ran.

The racers gave chase, the crowd gave a cheer!
And the slow little turtle, he brought up the rear.

Around the first bend, and under a tree,
Cookie Monster saw something that filled him with glee!

"A basket of cookies! Me think they're for me!
Me think me should have one. Or maybe have three!"

A basket again, this time filled with duckies!
Was it left there for Ernie? Or was he just lucky?

The turtle crawled past, just keeping his pace.
"Slow and steady," he said, "will win me this race."

Way up ahead, and just off the path,
Bert spotted some pigeons. They were having a bath.

He stopped there to greet them. Then he noticed the treats!
There were eggs by his head. There were eggs by his feet!

Leading the race, Big Bird had to wonder,
"What happened to Bunny? He's faster than thunder!"

But then, up ahead, he caught sight of a nest,
and he thought to himself, "Why not have a rest?"

With Big Bird asleep, the Count spied his chance,
while Zoe had stopped to make time for a dance!

She twirled by a maypole with ribbons galore.
With some help from her friends, she made a dance floor!

There was just one more hill, and a few turns to go.
The Count started smiling. He would put on a show!

The crowd cheered and whistled. Their excitement, it mounted!
But then Count saw a castle, and eggs to be counted.

On went the race, as the finish grew nearer…
but Grover was stopped by a bright, shiny mirror.

He twisted and turned, he stared and he gaped—
look at that hero, with his helmet and cape!

Elmo took first, with a spurt of full speed…
but a shiny toy truck cost him the lead!

The turtle crawled on, and broke through the line.
With no one in sight, it was his turn to shine!

"Turtle's the winner!" Big Bird called with a bellow,
and Count led a chorus of "Jolly Good Fellow."

And as for the bunny? He crossed the line last,
but he gave a sly wink of his eye as he passed.

For back at the park was a wonderful scene
of lollipops, chocolates, and pink jelly beans!

A big celebration of colorful treats.
A gift from the bunny, for Sesame Street!

Cover and internal design © 2017 by Sourcebooks, Inc.
Cover illustrations © Sesame Workshop
Text by Craig Manning
Illustrations by Ernest Kwiat

Published by Sourcebooks Jabberwocky, an imprint of Sourcebooks, Inc.
P.O. Box 4410, Naperville, Illinois 60567-4410
(630) 961-3900
Fax: (630) 961-2168
jabberwockykids.com
sourcebooks.com

Source of Production: Heshan City, Guangdong Province, China
Date of Production: October 2017
Run Number: 5010518

Printed and bound in China.
LEO 10 9 8 7 6 5 4 3 2